Struggling to Survive: The Lincolns' Difficult First Year in Illinois

Carolyn Harmon

Words Matter Publishing
P.O. Box 1190
Decatur, IL 62525
www.wordsmatterpublishing.com

ISBN 13: 978-1-962467-86-5

Library of Congress Catalog Card Number: 2025939436

Preface

Since childhood, I've been fascinated by stories of blizzards. Growing up, I experienced the Chicago-area blizzard of 1967. In that legendary storm, northwest Indiana saw even more snow than Chicago, thanks to Lake Michigan, with totals exceeding two feet. The relentless winds created drifts as high as six feet, leaving us housebound for several days. My uncle, with his brand-new snowmobile, became the local hero, delivering food and necessities to stranded neighbors.

Another unforgettable event was the Blizzard of 1978, which devastated Illinois, Indiana, and Ohio. Central Illinois also endured a spring ice storm that year, leaving many without power for over a week. While these weather disasters were challenging, we were fortunate to have modern snowplows and snowmobiles to help us navigate. Imagine enduring weeks of isolation in a drafty cabin with limited food and dwindling firewood—that thought truly puts the harshness of those winters into perspective.

My fascination with Abraham Lincoln began when I read *Abe Lincoln Gets His Chance* in grade school. That early introduction led me to dive into Carl Sandburg's *Lincoln*, sparking a lifelong interest in one of history's most remarkable figures. Living in Springfield, Illinois, and volunteering at the Abraham Lincoln Presidential Library and Museum have only deepened my admiration for him and my connection to his legacy.

Acknowledgments

I must thank Dr. Michael Burlingame, Dr. James Cornelius, Mark Sorensen, Tara McAndrew, my son, Nathan, and my grandchildren, for their review and comments. Steve Bean provided me with resources about Macon County and the Hanks family.

Table of Contents

Introduction

Many books have been written about Abraham Lincoln's early life, but not all of them tell the full story. Some skip over his first year in Illinois entirely, while others mention it without really explaining how tough that year was for Lincoln and his family. This time in his life was full of challenges, but it also shaped the man Lincoln would become.

During that first year in Illinois, Lincoln did some remarkable things. He gave his very first public speech and even wrote his first legal document! At just 21 years of age, he was able to earn money for himself for the first time.

Lincoln didn't have to move to Illinois with his family. He could have stayed behind in Indiana or gone off on his own to start a new life somewhere else. But he chose to stay with his family, helping them make the difficult move and settle into their new home. That year wasn't easy—it was filled with hard work, setbacks, and uncertainty.

So, what was it about Abraham Lincoln that helped him and his family get through such a tough time? What kind of people or connections helped them stay strong and keep going?

As you read, you'll learn how Lincoln's determination, kindness, and resilience helped him overcome challenges and set the foundation for his incredible journey toward becoming one of the most famous leaders in history.

CHAPTER 1

Moving Again

When Abraham Lincoln was 21 years old, his family decided to move to Illinois. Abraham could have gone off on his own—he was old enough and had already traveled to exciting places like New Orleans. But instead, he chose to help his family. Abraham was dependable and loyal, always putting others first. He had no idea how hard the next year would be, but years later, he described it as "one of the three eras of unusual hardship and misery."

Abraham's cousin, John Hanks, had already moved to Macon County, Illinois, with his large family in 1828. He had convinced Thomas Lincoln, Abraham's father, and Dennis Hanks, another family member, that Illinois was a great place to live. They hoped to escape the "milk sick" illness that had killed Abraham's mother, Nancy Hanks Lincoln, and start fresh, so it seemed like the perfect time to leave. Thomas and Dennis sold everything they could and packed up their belongings. They made covered wagons pulled by oxen to carry what they needed for the journey. Abraham even bought small items like needles, pins, and buttons to sell to people they met along the way. He later wrote to a friend that he doubled his money—proof of his creativity and business smarts!

The group moving to Illinois included 13 people: Abraham, his stepmother Sarah, her son John Johnston, and her daughters with their husbands and children. Leaving Indiana wasn't easy for Abraham. He said goodbye to his friends, as well as the graves of his mother and his sister Sarah, who had died giving birth to her first child.

The family left Indiana on March 1, hoping to have enough time to build a house and plant crops before winter. They used two or three covered wagons, and the trip took two long weeks. Traveling in 1830 was no simple task!

Figure 1: A road sign north of Petersburg, Indiana marking the Buffalo Trace

The roads they traveled were rough paths called "traces," which were made by buffalo and used by settlers. They likely started on the Yellow Banks Trace and then joined the Buffalo Trace, which led them to Vincennes, Indiana. The roads were muddy, and the ground froze at night and thawed during the day, making it tough for the wagons to move. They often got stuck, and everyone had to work together to pry them loose. Abraham would later say it was a "slow and tiresome journey."

Sometimes, they had to cut tree branches to clear the path. "Corduroy roads" made of logs made for a bumpy ride. Flooded rivers and creeks with no bridges made traveling even harder. They had to wade through icy water or risk losing their wagons to strong currents. Dennis Hanks later said they nearly lost the wagons when crossing the Kaskaskia River in Illinois. Sleeping outside in the freezing cold only made the journey harder.

Despite the challenges, Abraham kept everyone's spirits up. He told jokes and stories along the way. Dennis Hanks said, "Abe cracked a joke every time he cracked a whip." Abraham's sense of humor helped the group push through the difficult journey. Dennis also admired Abraham's cleverness, saying, "Abe found a way out of every tight place while the rest of us were standing around scratching our heads."

Abraham was also known for his kindness, especially to animals. One day, his little dog fell into an icy stream. The dog struggled to get out, but the ice was too thin. Abraham couldn't stand the thought of losing his dog, so he jumped out of the wagon, waded into the freezing water, and rescued him. Abraham later told a friend, "I could not endure the idea of abandoning even a dog." He carried the shivering dog back to the wagon, where the dog's happy jumps and wagging tail made it all worth it.

LINCOLN CROSSING THE STREAM WITH THE DOG.

Figure 2: Lincoln rescues his dog

This journey was full of challenges, but Abraham's loyalty, humor, and kindness helped his family through it. It showed the qualities that would later make him a great leader.

CHAPTER 2

Illinois

Figure 3: Lincoln Trail Memorial, Lawrenceville, Illinois. Located at the place where Lincoln and his family entered Illinois.

After many tiring days on the trail, the group finally reached the Wabash River near Vincennes. They likely crossed the river on a ferry, a large flatboat used to carry people, wagons, and oxen across the water. The Lincoln family was now in Illinois!

Years later, Indiana and Illinois marked the path the Lincolns probably traveled as part of the Lincoln Heritage Trail. They went by towns like Lickskillet, Loafers Station, Polk Patch, Dead Man's Grove, Purgatory Bottom and Paradise. The family continued their journey on the Paris-Springfield Road. There is a sign at Sand Creek Park south of Decatur, Illinois that explains this part of their journey.

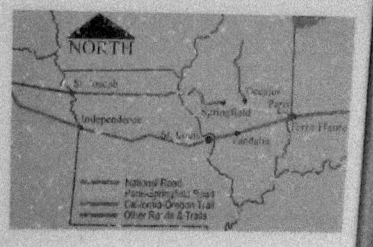

The Paris-Springfield Road
In the 1820's, the Illinois State Legislature authorized the laying out of a number of state roads into and across the interior of the state. The Paris-Springfield Road (1826) was one of the first joining the Middle Sangamon Valley with the National Road at Terre Haute, Indiana.

Figure 4: A section of the Paris-Springfield-Road in Sand Creek Park south of Decatur

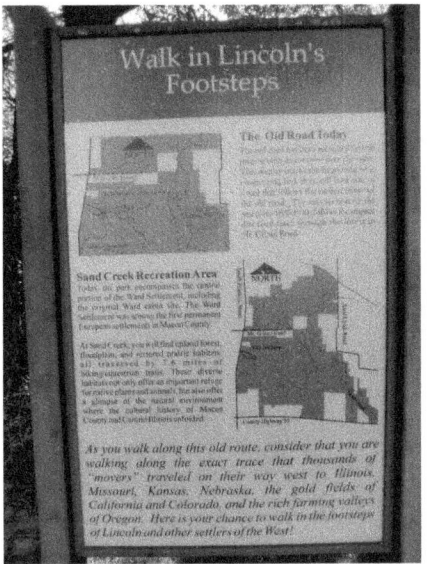

Figure 5: A sign in Sand Creek Park about the Paris-Springfield Road and the Lincoln journey

They probably crossed the Sangamon River at Ward's Ferry, just before arriving in the small town of Decatur. In downtown Decatur today, there's even a sign marking the spot where Abraham and his family stopped.

Figure 6: A Looking for Lincoln sign to commemorate the Lincoln family's arrival in Decatur. It includes a picture of the statue located at Millikin University about the same event.

When they reached Decatur, Abraham's cousin John Hanks was there to greet them. He had already prepared the way by cutting logs so the family could build a cabin. John guided the tired group to their new land, a bluff overlooking the Sangamon River.

Figure 7: A plaque located where people think the Lincoln cabin was located at Lincoln Trail Homestead State Park and Memorial west of Decatur, Illinois

Everyone worked together to build their new home. First, they built a small log cabin to live in. Then, they added a smokehouse for preserving meat and a barn for the animals. Of course, they also built an outhouse—it was an important part of every pioneer home! Their new cabin was simple and sturdy, made from the logs John had prepared. It wasn't fancy, but it gave them shelter from the cold and wind.

Even though their journey to Illinois was over, the hard work was just beginning. Abraham and his family had to build their new life from the ground up, one log and one task at a time.

CHAPTER 3

The Railsplitter

Figure 8: A drawing of Lincoln, the Railsplitter with a split rail fence

When Abraham and his family arrived in Illinois, they had to work hard to prepare the land for planting crops. Abraham split wooden rails to build fences around the area where they would plant their corn. Once the work on their own land was finished, Abraham began helping neighbors with their farm work. He often split rails with his cousin, John Hanks.

The wooden fence rails Abraham made looked sturdy and strong, just like the ones you can see today at New Salem State Park. They were used to build fences that kept animals out of the fields and protected crops from being trampled.

One of the neighbors Abraham worked for was a man named William Warnick. While working there, Abraham even wrestled one of the local men and won! Wrestling not only gave him a chance to show his strength, but it also helped him earn respect and make new friends.

Years later, in 1860, when Abraham ran for president, John Hanks brought one of the rails Abraham had supposedly split to the Republican Convention in Decatur. That's when people started calling Abraham "The Railsplitter," a nickname that reminded everyone of his humble beginnings and hard work.

Abraham also worked for his cousin, Mary Miller, to earn fabric for new clothes. Mary was John Hanks' sister, and she offered Abraham one yard of "homespun" cloth for every 400 rails he split. Abraham needed a lot of fabric, so he had to split over 1,000 rails! Her nephew, Dunham Wright, later said it took Abraham three whole days to split that many.

Figure 9: The type of clothing Lincoln wore at New Salem. From the Abraham Lincoln Presidential Museum, Springfield, Illinois

Thanks to his hard work, Abraham was able to take care of himself and earn what he needed. The clothes he wore back then were simple and practical. You can see an outfit similar to what Abraham would have worn on display at the Abraham Lincoln Presidential Library and Museum in Springfield, Illinois.

Abraham's strength, determination, and willingness to work hard made him self-sufficient and respected by those around him. These early experiences helped shape the leader he would one day become.

CHAPTER 4

First Speech and Cousin John

Abraham Lincoln gave his very first political speech in the summer of 1830 in downtown Decatur. A group of people had gathered to listen to politicians speak. When they were finished, Abraham's cousin, John Hanks, had an idea. He turned over a crate and said, "Abe, you should give a speech!"

LINCOLN'S FIRST SPEECH

IN JUNE 1830 FARM HAND ABRAHAM LINCOLN WAS WORKING ON

the farm of his relation, William Hanks, located just a few blocks from the main square in Decatur. Suddenly, he heard a disturbance coming from the square. Hopping the fence and heading to the noise, Lincoln found people had gathered to listen to John Posey and William L. D. Ewing. Posey was in town to speak for his candidacy to the Illinois General Assembly. Posey then gave his speech, and at the end came a "*shout*." Seizing the moment, Lincoln's second cousin John Hanks claimed a man in the audience could "*beat that speech to death.*" Hanks called on Lincoln to come forward. Barefooted, Lincoln readily accepted, mounted a tree stump (or an upturned wooden box), and proceeded to give a speech defending the Whig Party and its leader, Henry Clay of Kentucky. Lincoln argued for the navigation of the Sangamon River, focusing on the clearing and widening of the river to allow for transportation of farm goods and products. After the speech was over, the cheering crowd signaled that Lincoln's speech had "*carried the day.*"

Figure 10: A statue and Looking for Lincoln sign in downtown Decatur, Illinois where Lincoln gave his first speech

Abraham stood on the crate and talked about how the Sangamon River could be improved to allow boats to transport goods to the Illinois River. His speech was clear and full of good ideas, and the crowd loved it! People even said it was the best speech of the day.

John Hanks played an important role in Abraham's life. He was always there to encourage and support him. John was described as "homespun and matter-of-fact," someone who was generous, honest, and trustworthy. Abraham loved and respected his cousin, and their friendship made a big difference in those early years.

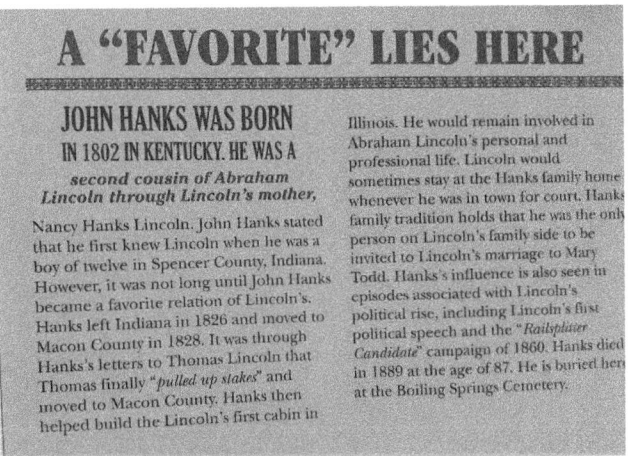

Figure 11: A Looking for Lincoln sign about John Hanks and Lincoln from Boiling Springs cemetery (where John is buried) north of Decatur, Illinois.

That same year, in December, Abraham wrote his first legal document. A stray horse, called an "estray mare," had been found, and Abraham helped with the official appraisal since he knew how to write and had community respect. The original document is now part of the Lincoln papers at the Abraham Lincoln Presidential Library.

With the support of a family like John Hanks and his own willingness to step up and try new things, Abraham was already showing signs of the leader he would one day become.

CHAPTER 5

Discouragement

As the fall of 1830 arrived, Abraham Lincoln and his community faced a terrible sickness called the "ague" or "Illinois shakes." This illness, which was likely malaria, came from the bites of pesky mosquitoes known as "gallinippers."

The disease was miserable. People would shake uncontrollably, suffer from burning fevers, and then experience chills so severe they couldn't get warm. Once the fever broke, they were left feeling weak and drained. One person described it as "a burning hot fever that lasted for hours. When you had a chill, you couldn't get warm, and when you had a fever, you couldn't get cool."

The Lincoln family suffered terribly. Abraham's father and stepmother both fell ill at the same time. Their small cabin was filled with sickness and sadness. Even Sarah's married daughter, who came to help care for them, was sick herself.

At the time, there was a treatment for malaria called Peruvian bark, which was mixed with whiskey to make a tonic. (Today, we know this bark as the source of quinine, a medicine used to fight malaria.) The Lincoln family bought Peruvian bark and whiskey from Renshaw's store in Decatur in August, hoping it would help.

The sickness was so bad that Abraham's father, Thomas Lincoln, made a vow: as soon as he was well enough to travel, he would move the family and "git out o' thar." But first, they had to recover, and that meant they couldn't leave until spring.

Unfortunately, even more challenges lay ahead for the Lincoln family before they could finally move on...

CHAPTER 6

The Deep Snow

The winter of 1830-31 brought the worst storm the Lincolns ever faced. Known as "The Deep Snow," it left six-foot-high drifts and temperatures that dropped to 20 degrees below zero. For two long months, freezing winds howled through the air, stinging skin and eyes and making it feel even colder. Snow blew into their small cabin through cracks between the logs, under the door, and even down the chimney.

At Lincoln Trail Homestead State Park, there are signs that show what the family endured during that harsh winter. One drawing even shows their tiny cabin buried in the snow!

Figure 12: A drawing of a cabin buried in the "Deep Snow". This is part of a Looking for Lincoln sign at Lincoln Trail Homestead State Park and Memorial.

Food and firewood became scarce as the storm dragged on. Corn left in the fields was hard to gather, and wild animals were nearly impossible to find. Trees were covered in thick layers of snow and ice, making it difficult to chop wood for the fire. Can you imagine being stuck in a tiny, cold, and dark cabin with almost no food for days on end?

Lincoln and his cousin John Hanks tried to help their family by traveling several miles to a mill to grind corn. It must have been a dangerous and exhausting trip. When someone asked how things were on their side of the river, they admitted they had run out of corn and were depending on neighbors for help.

Figure 13: Lincoln struggling through the frozen Sangamon River

One of Abraham's most difficult moments came when he crossed the frozen Sangamon River to ask a neighbor, William Warnick, for food. As he crossed, the ice broke, and his feet got soaked in the freezing water. He still had to walk two miles to the Warnick cabin, where Mrs. Warnick treated his frostbitten feet with a mixture of goose grease, skunk oil, and rabbit fat. Abraham stayed at the Warnick house for at least a week to recover.

While recuperating, he read law books owned by Mr. Warnick, who was the sheriff of Macon County. Abraham had built a good friendship with the Warnicks during the summer and fall when he had worked for them, and they were happy to help him in his time of need.

Despite the harsh winter, Abraham's kindness and willingness to help his neighbors didn't go unnoticed. According to DW Bartlett, Lincoln was well-liked because he helped others during those difficult months. He was always ready to give—and receive—help when it was needed.

Years later, survivors of this harsh winter became known as "snowbirds" by the Old Settlers' Association. Abraham Lincoln was proud to be one of them.

YEARS AFTER THE WINTER of the Deep Snow, many Illinois counties that had been established before that Winter formed their own Old Settlers' Association. These associations' main goals were to plan and stage reunions; gather and compile county histories; and participate in civic affairs. A person qualified as an "old settler" by virtue of having lived in Illinois during that benchmark Winter of the Deep Snow. Since Abraham Lincoln had lived in Macon County through that Winter, he qualified as an "old settler." He became a charter member of the Sangamon County Old Settlers' Association when it was formed in 1859.

Figure 14: Lincoln became a snowbird. Part of the Looking for Lincoln sign at Lincoln Trail State Park and Memorial

Even though Abraham spent less time with his father and stepmother that year because he was working for neighbors, he was always there when they needed him. His stepmother, Sarah Bush Johnston Lincoln, shared a close bond with Abraham, because she had encouraged and supported him when he was younger. He continued to care for her throughout her life, showing the same loyalty and kindness that defined his character.

Figure 15: Sarah Bush Johnston Lincoln,
Lincoln's beloved stepmother

CHAPTER 7

Parting Ways

When the long winter of deep snow finally came to an end, it was time for Abraham Lincoln to start a new chapter in his life. He decided to part with his father, and stepmother. Along with his cousin John Hanks and his stepbrother John Johnston, Abraham took on a job delivering a boatload of supplies to New Orleans for a man named Denton Offut. This trip would eventually lead Abraham to the small village of New Salem, where his life would change forever.

As for Thomas and Sarah Lincoln, they decided to leave Macon County and head back toward Indiana in the spring. Along the way, they stopped near Charleston, Illinois, where Sarah's sister lived. Instead of continuing to Indiana, they settled in the area, where they built a cabin. That cabin still stands today at the Lincoln Log Cabin State Historic Site near Lerna, Illinois.

Sarah's daughters, who had traveled with the family to Illinois, lived nearby with their husbands, Dennis Hanks and Squire Hall. After their trip to New Orleans, John Johnston married. He also stayed close to Thomas and Sarah. In the years to come, John often wrote letters to Abraham, asking for financial help when times were tough.

Figure 16: Dennis Hanks, Lincoln's cousin.

Dennis Hanks, who had been part of the family's journey to Illinois, shared stories about his life with Abraham in an 1889 interview. His daughters, Harriet Chapman and Sarah Jane Dowling, also shared their memories of traveling to Illinois as children. Harriet was just four years old, and Sarah Jane was eight during the 1830 trip. Their stories helped preserve the history of those early pioneer days.

Even as Abraham moved on to new adventures, the family he left behind remained connected, and their experiences in Illinois continued to shape their lives. For Abraham, parting ways with his family marked the beginning of a journey that would take him toward the man and leader the world would one day know.

CHAPTER 8

Lincoln's Resilience

Abraham Lincoln's first year in Illinois was filled with challenges, but he endured because of his remarkable qualities. He was dependable, patient, and creative. His hard work made him self-sufficient, and his kindness to both people and animals earned him the respect of those around him.

Lincoln had a wonderful sense of humor that others appreciated, and his practical intelligence helped him solve problems. He relied on the support of his family, including his stepmother Sarah and his cousin John Hanks. He also formed strong friendships with people like the Warnicks, who helped him during tough times.

The historian Ida Tarbell once said, "His strength won him popularity, but his good nature, his wit, his skill in debate, and his stories were even more effective in gaining him goodwill." People genuinely liked being around Abraham, and his personality drew others to him.

In July 1860, Lincoln shared these encouraging words: "Let no feeling of discouragement prey upon you, and in the end, you are sure to succeed." This message perfectly captures the resilience and determination that defined his character throughout his life.

Appendices

A. Lincoln Heritage Trail

Here is a map of the route from Indiana to Illinois in case you want to travel the trail.

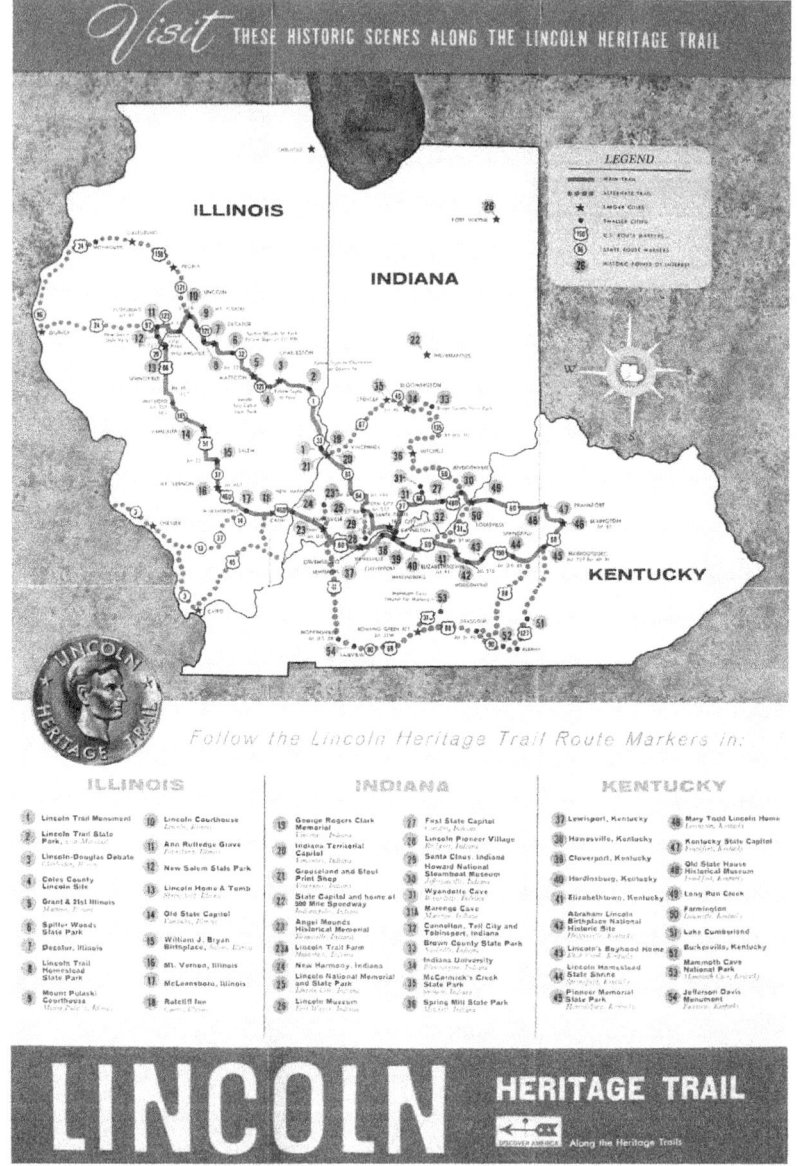

Figure 17: A map of the Lincoln Heritage Trail

Present-day road signs let you know you are on the trail.

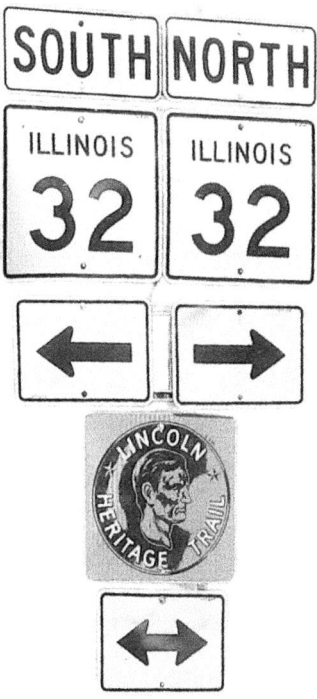

Figure 18: A road sign that has the Lincoln
Heritage Trail symbol.

B. What happened to the cabin?

Figure 19: John and Dennis Hanks in front of the Lincoln cabin
in 1865 before they took it apart.

The cabin was used by other people and possibly as a school until Lincoln's death. In 1865, John and Dennis Hanks and James Shoaff (Dennis's son-in-law) moved the cabin to Chicago to display at the Chicago Sanitary Fair. This meant taking the cabin apart and reassembling it. The *Chicago Tribune* and a *Voice of the Fair* publication explained about the cabin. Illinois Governor Oglesby authenticated the cabin. John Hanks said that half of the money he made would be donated to the Fair to help Civil War soldiers.

The cabin was then shipped to Boston and New York for display. It is unclear what happened to the cabin after that. One theory is that it was lost at sea, being shipped to Europe.

References

Atkinson, Eleanor. *The Boyhood of Lincoln*. New York: Double-day, Page & Co., 1909.

Bartlett, D. W. *The Life and Public Services of Honorable Abraham Lincoln*. New York: Derby & Jackson, 1860.

Burlingame, Michael. *Abraham Lincoln: A Life*. Unedited manuscript. Galesburg, IL: Knox College Lincoln Studies Center, 2008.

Cavanagh, Frances. *Abe Lincoln Gets His Chance*. New York: Scholastic, 1959.

Coleman, Charles. *Abraham Lincoln and Coles County, Illinois*. Lanham, MD: Scarecrow Press, 1955.

Davis, Edwin. "Lincoln and Macon County, Illinois, 1830–1831." *Journal of the Illinois State Historical Society*, Vol. 25, No. 12, April–June, 1932, pp. 63–107.

Gridley, Eleanor. *The Story of Abraham Lincoln: Or the Journey from the Log Cabin to the White House*. Chicago: Wabash Publishing Co., 1900.

Kyle, Otto. *Abraham Lincoln in Decatur*. New York: Vantage Press, 1957.

Mansberger, Floyd. "Searching for the Thomas Lincoln Cabin." *Outdoor Illinois*, August, 2009.

McClellan McAndrew, Tara. "The Lincolns' First Home in Illinois: Decatur Site Gets New Study and a Makeover." *Illinois Times*, February 11, 2009.

North, Sterling. *Abraham Lincoln: Log Cabin to White House.* New York: Landmark Books, 1956.

Sandburg, Carl. *Abraham Lincoln: The Prairie Years.* New York: Harcourt, Brace & Co., 1926.

Smith, John. *History of Macon County Illinois: From Its Organization to 1876.* Springfield, IL: Rokker's Printing House, 1876.

Tarbell, Ida. *The Early Life of Abraham Lincoln.* New York: S.S. McClure Ltd., 1896.

Thayer, William. *The Pioneer Boy and How He Became President.* Boston: Walker, Wise and Co., 1863.

Thompson, Charles. "The Lincoln Way." *The Alumni Quarterly of the University of Illinois*, Vol. VII, Oct. 1913, No. 4, pp. 271–276.

Weik, Jesse,(1922) ed. by Michael Burlingame. *The Real Lincoln: A Portrait.* Lincoln, NE: University of Nebraska Press, 2002.

Whitney, Henry. *Lincoln the Citizen (February 12, 1809 – March 4, 1861).* New York: Current Publishing Company, 1907.

Photo and Illustration Credits

Cover
1 Indiana road sign
2 Gridley, Eleanor
3 Illinois Department of Natural Reources
4-5 Macon County Conservation District
6 Looking for Lincoln
7 Illinois Department of Natural Resources
8 Harper Winslow
9 Abraham Lincoln Presidential Library and Museum
10 Decatur and Macon County Heritage Commission
11-12 Looking for Lincoln
13 Harper Winslow
14 Looking for Lincoln
15 National Park Service
16 National Park Service
17 state of Illinois
18 Illinois road sign
19 Library of Congress

For More Information

Abraham Presidential Library and Museum, Springfield, IL: presidentlincoln.illinois.gov, Facebook

Buffalo Trace in Indiana: bt.indianashistoricpathways.org

Decatur, IL Convention and Visitors Bureau: decaturcvb.com/abraham-lincoln-decatur

Decatur IL Public Library Local History Room: decaturlibrary.org

Friends of Lincoln Trail Homestead State Park and Memorial: lincolntrailhomest.wixsite.com, Facebook

Illinois Department of Natural Resources dnr.illinois.gov, Facebook

    Lincoln Trail Homestead State Park and Memorial near Harristown, IL

    Lincoln Trail State Memorial, near Lawrenceville, IL

Looking for Lincoln: www.lookingforlincoln.com, Facebook

Macon County Conservation District: www.maconccd.org

Macon County Historical Society Museum: www.mchsde-catur.org

www.ingramcontent.com/pod-product-compliance
Lightning Source LLC
Chambersburg PA
CBHW051335120626
46547CB00016B/2552